This is for Madeleine and Amelia, and our friend, Lew.
—K. K.

To those who missed the boat.
—M. G.

Atheneum Books for Young Readers
An imprint of Simon & Schuster Children's Publishing Division
1230 Avenue of the Americas
New York, New York 10020

Book design by Sonia Chaghatzbanian
The text of this book was set in KentuckyFried.
The illustrations were rendered in watercolor.

Printed in Mexico

10 9 8 7 6 5 4 3 2 1

Library of Congress Cataloging-in-Publication Data

Kuskin, Karla.
The Animals and the Ark / Karla Kuskin & Michael Grejniec.–1st ed.
p.   cm.
ISBN 0-689-83095-5
1. Noah's ark–Juvenile literature. [1. Noah's ark.
2. Bible stories.–O.T.] I. Grejniec, Michael, ill. II. Title.
BS658 .K87 2001
222'.1109505–dc21   00-040148

FIRST
EDITION

The Animals and the Ark

written by
Karla Kuskin

illlustrated by
Michael Grejniec

Atheneum Books for Young Readers
New York London Toronto Sydney Singapore

The sun was bright.
The earth was dry.
Noah looked up and scanned the sky.
He said, "I think it's going to pour.
It's going to rain and rain some more.

The sun will dim,
the day turn dark,
with all that rain
I'll need an Ark."

← This is the Ark.

These are the sons of Noah who built the Ark as he told them to.

Shem was the eldest,

Ham was last,

Japheth wore yellow.

They all worked fast.

They sawed and hammered with might and main

in order to finish before the rain.

They cut down trees and peeled the bark

and made themselves
a lovely Ark

WELCOME

for

the fowl of the air

for the mole from his hole

and the lynx from his lair

for rats

and cats

and calves and cows

for rams
and lambs

and snakes

and sows

and every single kind of beast

from **moose**

to goose

from most
to least.

They came from the sands.

They came from
the skies,
with growling and prowling
and animal cries.

They came from the plains. They came from the hills.

The elephants came with the whippoorwills.

They crept
and flew,

they skipped
and hopped

and when they
got to the Ark

they stopped.

Then Shem put down a plank for stairs
and Ham said he would count the pairs

and Japheth made them wipe their feet
and gave them each a bite to eat.

16

The rain came down
and the sky got dark.
The animals huddled
inside the Ark.

It splashed and splattered.
It splithered and splushed.

A few bats whined
but were quickly hushed.

The water got higher and covered the valleys.
It made deep lakes in the highways and alleys.
The water kept rising and covered the hills.
It covered the iris and daffodils.
It covered the trees and the mountain peaks
and the water kept rising for weeks and weeks.

The Ark no longer was on the ground;
it rose with the water and floated around
and all of the animals stayed inside
and ate and slept and played inside
at "Hide-and-Seek" and "Make a Nice Motion"
while the whole wide world was covered with ocean.

The rain rained on
and they all got bored.

The elephant honked
when the antelope snored.

Then all of a sudden
just at the point

when the lioness ached in every joint,

when cattle were   lowing

and monkeys were squealing

and bats were bumping all over the ceiling,

when the air was hot

and the straw was damp

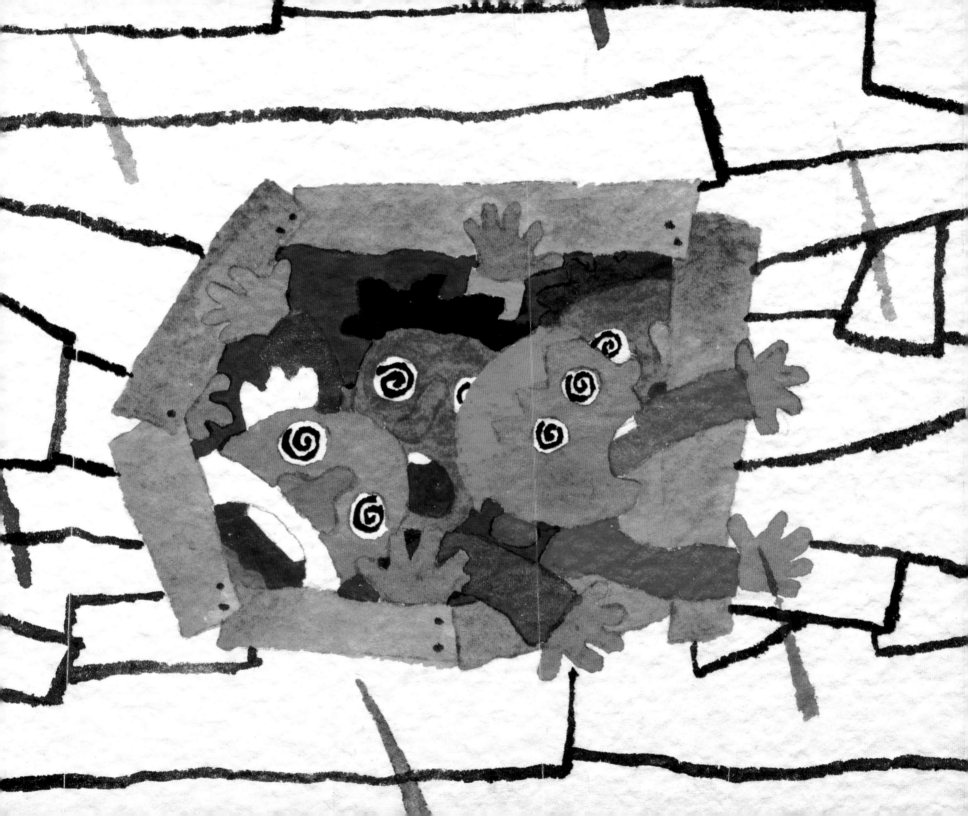

when Noah was helpless
and so was his crew

and a bad-tempered tiger developed a cramp,

when the fighting and crying were awful and fearful and all the small animals seemed to be tearful,

At PRECISELY THAT MOMENT

the sun broke

through!

And that, of course,
is the end of the poem.
They all got up
and they all went home.